Barbie™ AND THE ROCKERS™
THE FAN

By Teddy Slater

Illustrated by Tom Tierney

A GOLDEN BOOK • NEW YORK

Western Publishing Company, Inc., Racine, Wisconsin 53404

"New York!" cried Barbie.

"Chicago!" whooped Dee Dee.

"And don't forget Hollywood!" Diva chimed in. "This is going to be our best concert tour ever. Ten cities in twenty days, and every show is already sold out!"

"Yeah," said Derek. "Our publicity campaign really paid off. Especially the 'Weekend with The Rockers' contest. We must have gotten a million entries."

"I wonder what the winner's like," Ken mused. "Delia DeVoe...what a great name! Diva, Dana, Dee Dee, and Delia— sounds like she belongs with the band."

"Well," said Barbie, "we'll find out all about her when we get to Los Angeles. It won't be long now."

Meanwhile, in Los Angeles, Delia DeVoe had her mind on music, but not on The Rockers. She was too busy preparing for a performance of her own. In just three weeks she would be trying out for a place at the Los Angeles High School of Music and Art. The competition among violinists was expected to be fierce.

"I just wish you hadn't won that silly contest," Delia's mother said. "I hate to think of you missing a whole weekend of practice so close to your audition."

"Oh, Mother," Delia said, groaning, "I've been practicing the violin three hours a day for the last five years. If I'm not ready now, I never will be. As a matter of fact, I'm sick of practicing. I could use a break."

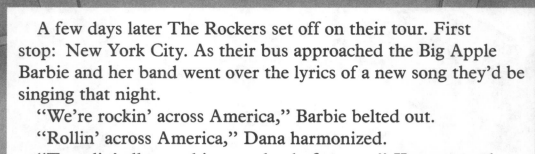

A few days later The Rockers set off on their tour. First stop: New York City. As their bus approached the Big Apple Barbie and her band went over the lyrics of a new song they'd be singing that night.

"We're rockin' across America," Barbie belted out.

"Rollin' across America," Dana harmonized.

"Travelin' all over this great land of ours..." Ken crooned.

A huge crowd had gathered outside The Rockers' hotel to welcome the band to New York. While the roadies unloaded the sound equipment Barbie and her friends signed autographs.

"Will you be at the concert tonight?" Barbie asked a girl.

"I wouldn't miss it for the world," she said. "I have all your records. They're really great. And I bet you'll be even greater in person."

At the concert that night, Barbie and The Rockers didn't disappoint the girl, or any of the thousands of other teens who packed the arena. The Rockers gave their best performance ever. And the enthusiastic audience kept them onstage until well after midnight, demanding one encore after another.

It seemed that Barbie had barely closed her eyes when it was time to get up—and back on the road—again. Next stop: Philadelphia.

Heading west, The Rockers performed in one city after another...Cleveland, Detroit, Chicago, Des Moines. And each concert was better than the one before.

When the group finally pulled into
Los Angeles at the end of the tour,
they were greeted by the usual crowd
of fans, plus one very special fan—
Delia DeVoe.

The Rockers whisked Delia away with them to a press conference, where Barbie introduced her to newspaper and TV reporters and described the contest.

Delia's prizewinning essay, "What Music Means to Me," had earned her two fun-filled days as The Rockers' special guest. She'd accompany them everywhere and wind up the weekend with a front-row seat at the band's final concert on Sunday night.

Early the next morning, The Rockers took Delia along for their costume fitting. The young violinist was dazzled by the glittering clothes and couldn't help comparing them with her own skirt and sweater. She felt painfully plain—especially when Derek's eyes lit up at the sight of Diva modeling one of the outfits.

Then Barbie and The Rockers were off to the local television station, where they would be appearing on an afternoon talk show.

While watching the program on a monitor in the control room, Delia sat openmouthed as Barbie told the host about the time the group sang for the President and the First Lady. The others had exciting tales, too.

But Delia most enjoyed listening to and watching Derek. He certainly looked handsome on TV.

The next day was packed with activity as Delia accompanied
The Rockers to a dress rehearsal, a charity auction, and a gala
publicity party. The weekend seemed to be flying by.

"If only it would never end," Delia thought. Suddenly her life
at home seemed very dull.

Sitting in her front-row seat at the concert that night, Delia wished she were even closer. In fact, she didn't want to be in the audience at all. She wanted to be onstage with The Rockers and already felt like part of the group. Barbie and the other girls seemed like big sisters, Ken was like an older brother, and as for Derek...well, he was something special.

It didn't take much imagination for Delia to picture herself as a member of The Rockers. After all, she was a musician. With so many years of violin study behind her, the guitar wouldn't be too hard to learn. She could get a tutor for her high school courses. And she wouldn't even have to change her name. It was perfect—Diva, Dana, Dee Dee, and *Delia*!

Delia could hardly wait for the concert to end. She was eager to share her thoughts with The Rockers. As soon as the final curtain came down she rushed backstage.

The band members listened in silence as Delia excitedly announced her plan to quit the violin and take up the guitar.

When she finally paused for breath, Derek said gently, "We've loved having you around this weekend, but I'm afraid you've gotten a false picture of our lives."

"That's right," Barbie agreed. "So far, all you've seen is the glamorous side of this business. The costume fittings, press conferences, and parties are all great fun, but there's more to it than that—a lot more.

"If you want to see how it really is, why don't you come to the R-N-R Studios tomorrow after school and sit in while we cut our new album."

When Delia showed up at the recording studio the next afternoon, Barbie and the band were in the middle of a song. Suddenly the chief engineer held up his hand and signaled the musicians to stop.

"Would you try that again from the top?" he asked. "I'm getting too much guitar and not enough piano."

The Rockers cheerfully started the song again. Two hours and fifteen tries later they were still happily at it. But Delia was exhausted just from listening. "This is worse than violin practice," she thought. "I had no idea playing rock and roll could be such hard work."

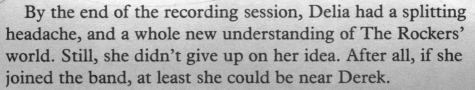

By the end of the recording session, Delia had a splitting headache, and a whole new understanding of The Rockers' world. Still, she didn't give up on her idea. After all, if she joined the band, at least she could be near Derek.

As the session was breaking up, Delia heard Derek say, "Got to run. I have a late date."

Suddenly she felt foolish for having imagined herself as his girlfriend. After all, her mother wouldn't even let her go out on a date yet.

Before Derek had a chance to run off, Delia stopped him and said, "Derek—Barbie—everyone—you were right. I had no idea what being a rock star was all about. For now I'll stick to what I already know—the violin. I'm sure going to miss you all, but I'll still be your number-one fan."

Barbie said, "Who knows? Maybe someday you'll play the guitar, too. Just don't walk away from something you're so good at.

"There will always be a front-row seat for you anytime The Rockers are in town," Barbie continued.

"And we'll expect you to return the favor when you're a famous violinist," Derek added with a wink. "Because we're all pretty big fans of yours, too!"